For Natasha, Sabrina and Jasmine – J.D.

First published 2001 by Macmillan Children's Books
This edition published 2016 by Macmillan Children's Books
an imprint of Pan Macmillan
20 New Wharf Road, London N1 9RR
Associated companies throughout the world
www.panmacmillan.com

ISBN 978-1-5098-1519-7

1 3 5 7 9 8 6 4 2

A CIP catalogue record for this book is available
from the British Library.

Read by Josie Lawrence
Produced by Anne Rosenfeld for RBA Productions, mixed by Joseph Degnan
Music by Chris Branch, based on the Room on the Broom Song by Julia Donaldson
Room on the Broom Song lyrics and melody copyright © Julia Donaldson 2002
Sung by Josie Lawrence

Printed in China

WRITTEN BY
JULIA DONALDSON

ILLUSTRATED BY
AXEL SCHEFFLER

Room on the Broom

MACMILLAN CHILDREN'S BOOKS

The witch had a cat
and a very tall hat,
And long ginger hair
which she wore in a plait.
How the cat purred
and how the witch grinned,
As they sat on their broomstick
and flew through the wind.

But how the witch wailed
and how the cat spat,
When the wind blew so wildly
it blew off the hat.

"Down!" cried the witch,
and they flew to the ground.
They searched for the hat
but no hat could be found.

Then out of the bushes
on thundering paws
There bounded a dog
with the hat in his jaws.

He dropped it politely,
then eagerly said
(As the witch pulled the hat
firmly down on her head),
"I am a dog, as keen as can be.
Is there room on the broom
for a dog like me?"

"Yes!" cried the witch,
and the dog clambered on.
The witch tapped the broomstick and
whoosh! they were gone.

O ver the fields and the
forests they flew.
The dog wagged his tail
and the stormy wind blew.
The witch laughed aloud
and held onto her hat,
But away blew the bow
from her long ginger plait!

Then out from a tree,
    with an ear-splitting shriek,
There flapped a green bird
    with the bow in her beak.
She dropped it politely
    and bent her head low,

"Down!" cried the witch,
    and they flew to the ground.
They searched for the bow
    but no bow could be found.

Then said (as the witch
   tied her plait in a bow),
"I am a bird,
   as green as can be.
Is there room on the broom
   for a bird like me?"

"Yes!" cried the witch,
   so the bird fluttered on.
The witch tapped the broomstick and
   whoosh! they were gone.

Over the reeds and the
        rivers they flew.
The bird shrieked with glee
        and the stormy wind blew.
They shot through the sky
        to the back of beyond.
The witch clutched her bow
        but let go of her wand.

"Down!" cried the witch,
        and they flew to the ground.
They searched for the wand
        but no wand could be found.

Then all of a sudden
    from out of a pond
Leapt a dripping wet frog
    with a dripping wet wand.
He dropped it politely,
    then said with a croak
(As the witch dried the wand
    on a fold of her cloak),
"I am a frog, as clean as can be.
Is there room on the broom
    for a frog like me?"
"Yes!" said the witch, so the frog
    bounded on.

The witch tapped the broomstick and
    whoosh! they were gone.
Over the moors and the
    mountains they flew.
The frog jumped for joy and . . .

. . . THE BROOM
SNAPPED IN TWO!

Down fell the cat and the dog
 and the frog.
Down they went tumbling
 into a bog.

The witch's half-broomstick
 flew into a cloud,
And the witch heard a roar
 that was scary and loud . . .

"I am a dragon, as mean as can be,
And I'm planning to have WITCH
        AND CHIPS for my tea!"
"No!" cried the witch,
        flying higher and higher.
The dragon flew after her,
        breathing out fire.
"Help!" cried the witch,
        flying down to the ground.
She looked all around
        but no help could be found.

The dragon drew nearer and,
        licking his lips,
Said, "Maybe this once
        I'll have witch without chips."

But just as he planned
to begin on his feast,
From out of a ditch
rose a horrible beast.
It was tall, dark and sticky,
and feathered and furred.
It had four frightful heads,
it had wings like a bird.
And its terrible voice,
when it started to speak,
Was a yowl and a growl
and a croak and a shriek.
It dripped and it squelched
as it strode from the ditch,
And it said to the dragon,
"Buzz off! –
THAT'S MY WITCH!"

The dragon drew back
   and he started to shake.
"I'm sorry!" he spluttered.
   "I made a mistake.
It's nice to have met you,
   but now I must fly."
And he spread out his wings
   and was off through the sky.

Then down flew the bird
   and down jumped the frog.
Down climbed the cat,
   and "Phew!" said the dog.
And, "Thank you, oh, thank you!"
   the grateful witch cried.
"Without you I'd be
   in that dragon's inside."

Then she filled up her cauldron
and said with a grin,
"Find something, everyone,
throw something in!"
So the frog found a lily,
the cat found a cone,
The bird found a twig
and the dog found a bone.

They threw them all in
and the witch stirred them well,
And while she was stirring
she muttered a spell.
"Iggety, ziggety, zaggety, ZOOM!"

Then out rose . . .

. . . A TRULY MAGNIFICENT BROOM!

With seats for the witch
    and the cat and the dog,
A nest for the bird and
    a shower for the frog.

"Yes!" cried the witch,
    and they all clambered on.
The witch tapped the broomstick and
    whoosh! they were gone.